Up From the Sea

Up From the Sea

LEZA LOWITZ

CROWN
New York

Text copyright © 2016 by Leza Lowitz
Jacket art and design by Ray Shappell
Hand lettering copyright © 2016 by Alison Carmichael

Lyrics translated from *"Tohoku Ondo"* by Ken Odajima and Hachiro Sato
copyright © 1965 by Kahoku Shimpo Publishing Co., used with permission
of the publisher and Sato Hachiro Memorial Museum.

Visit us on the Web! randomhouseteens.com

Educators and librarians, for a variety of teaching tools,
visit us at RHTeachersLibrarians.com

Library of Congress Cataloging-in-Publication Data
Lowitz, Leza.
Up from the sea / Leza Lowitz.—First edition.
pages cm.
Summary: A novel in verse about the March 2011 tsunami that sent
Japan into chaos, told from the point-of-view of Kai, a biracial teenaged boy.
ISBN 978-0-553-53474-0 (trade)—ISBN 978-0-553-53475-7 (lib. bdg.)—
ISBN 978-0-553-53476-4 (ebook)
1. Tohoku Earthquake and Tsunami, Japan, 2011—Juvenile fiction.
[1. Tohoku Earthquake and Tsunami, Japan, 2011—Fiction.
2. Racially mixed people—Fiction. 3. Japan—Fiction.] I. Title.
PZ7.L96548Up 2016 [Fic]—dc23 2014048672

Printed in the United States of America
10 9 8 7 6 5 4 3 2 1
First Edition

For Tohoku

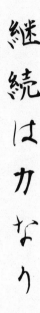

perseverance becomes its own kind of strength

JAPANESE SAYING

Preface

At 2:46 p.m. on Friday, March 11, 2011, a 9.0-magnitude earthquake struck the Tohoku region of Honshu, Japan, 231 miles northeast of Tokyo. It was the strongest temblor ever to hit that quake-prone country. It lasted six minutes. After the quake struck, a massive tsunami followed. The Pacific Ocean lifted from the seafloor and slammed into 300 miles of coastline. The tsunami—one of the largest ever recorded, with waves reaching up to 133 feet—swept five miles inland, destroying entire villages. The earthquake moved the main island of Japan eight feet east and shifted the Earth on its axis between four and ten inches. One hundred fifty-five miles up the coast from Tokyo, the six-reactor Fukushima Daiichi nuclear plant was also damaged, causing a dangerous nuclear meltdown. There were 11,106 aftershocks, many measuring over 7 on the Richter scale.

Approximately 15,889 people died, 6,152 were injured, and 2,601 people are still missing. And 127,290 buildings were destroyed, with a million more severely damaged in the Tohoku region, an area known for its rich history and folklore, delicious mackerel and oysters, the scenic beauty of the pine-studded islands of Matsushima, and the resilience of its people. Thousands in the affected areas are still living in temporary housing. It will take decades for the region to fully recover, but the strength and courage of the Tohoku people remain unshakable.

春

Spring

3

Adrift

MY TOWN—

Didn't love it,
didn't hate it—
it was just
where I lived.

In the back of my mind,
there was always New York,
where Dad lived a life
I could only imagine—
far from this sleepy town
with its ponds and pines,
temples and tea,
wooden houses
falling into each other
like sailors wobbly
from too much *sake*,
days as predictable
as the tides.

In the back of my mind,
I'd graduate from high school,
leave the place
Dad left
behind.

MARCH 11—

Mom rode her bike to the oyster farm,
pulled shell clusters from the ocean,
pried the oysters off the mother shells,
washed the sludge away.

Obaachan* picked wild ferns on the mountain.
Ojiichan† fixed a busted light on his sanma‡ boat.

Shin's dad washed his taxi in their garage,
bleached the seat covers white as bone.

Shin, Ryu, and I walked to school together—
Ryu juggling his soccer ball the whole way.

---

*   Obaachan—Grandma

†   Ojiichan—Grandpa

‡   sanma—mackerel

We planned to skateboard by the seawall
after school, but we never made it.

Just an ordinary spring morning,
ordinary fight with Mom.
Maybe she spoke to me in English
and I answered in Japanese—
don't even remember now.
Maybe I threw my dirty socks onto the floor
or left the toilet seat up again.

Whatever it was seems so stupid
at 2:46 p.m., when I'm sitting in math
waiting for the bell to ring

and the earth starts to shake.

I DO
....

what they've taught us since nursery school—
bring my knees to my chest, cover my head.

The desks rattle,
the window frames buckle,
the building creaks
from side to side,
no one runs out.

We laugh, thinking we'll
get out of school early,
thinking the quake will stop
like the others always have.

But the shaking continues,
stronger and stronger,
not caring at all
what we thought.

THE CLOCK

flies off the wall.
Time stops.
Windows shatter.

We dive under desks—
this time for real.
The earth jolts us over
and over.
It's like getting kicked up
from the ground
and thrown
from side to side
and punched

in the stomach
all at once.

Aki-*sensei* shouts:
Evacuate!
Evacuate!
his voice fierce,
urgent.

MY KNEES

shake,
my legs
shake,
my hands
shake,
but somehow
I manage
to stumble
out from under my desk,
stand up,
scramble to pull
the yellow vest
and hard hat
free,

put them on,
throw the
emergency pack
onto my back.

We rush out of the room—
all except for Keiko Inoue,
curled under her desk,
long legs tucked into
her chest,
frozen.

KEIKO! COME ON!

We've got to go! I shout.
She doesn't budge.
I reach out,
but she won't
take my hand.

Get up! Get UP!
NOW!

Her dark
brown eyes won't focus—
she's not there.

The wall cracks,
splits in half
with a groan.

Taro Nishi pushes me aside,
kicks over the desk,
scoops up Keiko,
slings her like a deer
over his broad shoulders.

So relieved
to be out
of the building—
then I look at Taro
carrying Keiko,
think:
Wish it had been me.

SCHOOL SWAYS AND TILTS,

playground cracks,
classroom crumbles,
cinder blocks shower,
sheets of wall collapse.

Roof buckles into itself,
tiles rain down

with chunks of concrete,
shards of glass.

In the distance,
water sloshes over
the edge of the pool.

I close my eyes,
pray I'll wake up
from this nightmare,
pray that everything
will be normal again.

LOUDSPEAKERS ANNOUNCE

Tsunami!
A tsunami is coming!

It's been drilled into us
since nursery school—

a tsunami always
follows a quake.

Still,
I never thought

I'd be
this close to one—
too close to one
right here,
right
now.

SIRENS

break through
the eerie silence.
Then Aki-*sensei* shouts:
Higher ground!
Get to higher ground!

Another quake
shakes the earth
beneath our feet,
jolts us sideways,
almost knocks us down.

LIKE A BULLET TRAIN

we speed off
toward the mountains
behind the school.

First straight lines,
then chaos,
scurrying toward safety.

I turn around,
keep my eye on Shin
behind me—
tall, thin Shin,
he says he's got my back.

Ryu's up ahead,
strong thighs pumping.
Hurry up, everyone! he shouts,
moving quick as lightning.

I'm fast, too.
That's what Coach Inoue
always said—
fastest boy in town—
gotta prove him right.

Gotta make it up the hill!
Come on!
We're going to be all right!
Ryu shouts, even though
everyone knows

the water will
be coming soon.

Dirt flying at our heels,
ocean at our backs,
we funnel our bodies
into narrow streets,
zigzag around rubble—
once-peaceful town
now a war zone.

ALMOST AT THE MOUNTAIN BASE—

fallen pine trees
block the path!
Can't get up
the mountain.

Can't go back.

Sky turns black,
then orange,
then red.

Clouds open up to
sudden rain.

Teachers huddle,
try to determine
the next-highest place.

FINGERS SHAKING,

I text Mom
to let her know
I'm okay.
But I don't say that.
Instead I ask
R u ok?

She texts back
right away.
R U? I'm fine.
I love you, Kai
& a heart
& smile.
I'm smiling, too—
only notice
that I'm
crying
when I taste salt
in my mouth.

SCCCCHHHLLLLLLLLLLLLLUUUUUU—

strange sound
rises from behind us
like a giant Slurpee
being sucked through
the biggest straw
in the world.

Let's go!
Aki-*sensei* shouts.
To the bridge!

Its span is high—
we'll be safe.

FIVE BLOCKS ACROSS TOWN

to the river—
just five blocks!

Must have run five times
that for soccer
every day
when I was
little.

But a huge black sheet of water
curls away
from the shore,
leaves the ocean floor
totally open
bare,
exposed—
like us. . . .

HEART POUNDING

legs pounding
head pounding

obstacle course of
crumbled buildings
chunks of pavement
rooftops strewn like train tracks
tracks buckled like busted rooftops
downed electric cables
splintered boards
upturned cars
ships on land
flattened trucks.

Each block
is like

a continent
to cross.

ANOTHER QUAKE

hurls us
into the air.

I look up at Ryu—
always the leader—
propelling me
with his motion.
Now
he's on the ground.

Shin is way behind—
gangly grasshopper legs
buckling in and out
like they always did
on the soccer field.

Can't go on!
Ryu groans.
You can do this! I stop,
reach for his hand,
pick him up and

drag him along,
legs pinwheeling.

Keep running!
Aki-*sensei* shouts,
shirt clinging
to his sweat-drenched back.

Gotta make it
to the bridge.

Gotta run
faster than we've
ever run,
faster than we
knew we could

because the
foaming
mass
is coming up
so fast
so strong
so soon—
too soon—
behind us.

Almost there!

BLACK MONSTER

raging,
smashing
into land,
exploding
in sky-high spray

snapping
crunching
crushing
everything
in its wake.

Horns beeping
cars swirling
water
sweeping up
busesstreetlampsshopsigns
homesbuildingstrees
even people.

WE MAKE IT

to the bridge—

spanning out
over the river

like the wings
of an angel.
Safe!

But the water
makes it, too,
churns
around the piers
thrashes
into the railings
surges
over the railings
sweeps
onto the deck
charges
right up
to where
we're
standing.

SHIN! RYU! AKI-SENSEI! KEIKO!

R
U
N
!

BRIDGE HEAVES

to the left
then
splits
in
half
as if concrete
and steel
were
balsa
wood.

We go
down
with it.

INTO THE WAVE

f
r
e
e
f
a
l
l

Sucked under
the freezing
black mass—

have to
breathe.

Have to
break free.

Have to
get away
from the
foul-smelling
eye-stinging

throat-burning
monster.

THWAAACK!
Slammed so hard
my nose
cracks,
tinny taste—
blood
in my mouth.

I reach out,
hold on to the tree,
scramble up
hand over hand,
thighs squeeze
and release,
squeeze and release
up up up
like the monkey
Mom always
said I was.

10 feet
20 feet

30 feet
40 feet

Don't know
how high I am,
don't care.

Just hope
I'm higher
than the
next wave.

But the monster
rears
up again.

THE PINE TREE

bends,
sways,
bows
low
to the
ground.

Waterwaterwaterwaterwaterwater
up to my feet

up to my thighs
up to my chest
up to my head
up to my mouth
just want
air.

CAN'T GIVE UP

can't
give in
can't
give way
can't
go under
so cold
so cold
can't
breathe
can't
do
anything.

SILENT

underwater
world.

Then

Mom's voice:
Kai
Kai
Kai . . .

Afloat

FACEDOWN

in the sludge—
bruised
and battered.

Don't know
where I am
or how long
I've been here,
shivering,
shaking,
coughing up
sand
dirt
seawater
sludge
until I'm
empty.

clothes in strips—
Principal Kunihara.

You OK?
Where's Shin, Ryu?
I cough out.

Don't know . . .
His once-booming voice
now a whisper.

Hand on my back,
he guides me
up the hill
to the junior high.

My head hurts.
My body hurts.
Where's Mom?
Where's everyone?

Where's my favorite
ramen place?

What happened
to the vegetable market
the fish shop
the tofu maker
the video store?

BIG BLACK DIRT

BIG BLACK DIRT BIG BLACK DIRT BIG BLACK
DIRT BIG BLACK DIRT BIG BLACK DIRT BIG
BLACK DIRT BIG BLACK DIRT BIG BLACK
DIRT BIG BLACK DIRT BIG BLACK DIRT BIG
BLACK DIRT BIG BLACK DIRT BIG BLACK DIRT
BIG BLACK DIRT BIG BLACK DIRT BIG BLACK
DIRT BIG BLACK DIRT BIG BLACK DIRT BIG
BLACK DIRT BIG BLACK DIRT BIG BLACK DIRT
BIG BLACK DIRT BIG BLACK DIRT BIG BLACK
DIRT BIG BLACK DIRT BIG BLACK DIRT BIG
BLACK DIRT BIG BLACK DIRT BIG BLACK DIRT
BIG BLACK DIRT BIG BLACK DIRT BIG BLACK
DIRT BIG BLACK DIRT BIG BLACK DIRT BIG
BLACK DIRT BIG BLACK DIRT BIG BLACK DIRT
BIG BLACK DIRT BIG BLACK DIRT BIG BLACK
DIRT BIG BLACK DIRT BIG BLACK DIRT BIG
BLACK DIRT BIG BLACK DIRT BIG BLACK DIRT

What happened to
my town?

IN THE AUDITORIUM,

people huddle together
on the floor,
rocking back
and forth.

I'm too scared
to ask the question
that matters most.

BUT I NEED TO KNOW,

so I go looking
face to face—
neighbors
townspeople
strangers
old
young
wet,
bleeding,
shaking.

None of them
are
Mom,
Ojiichan,
Obaachan,
Shin,
or
Ryu. . . .

MY EYES LAND

on Aki-*sensei*—
brown face now ashen,
big man now small,
bent over like a bonsai.

You're okay! he says,
relieved.
No, I say.
I gotta go find
my mom
and grandparents!
Now!

THEN WE'RE SLAMMED

from side to side
like we're a bone
the earth keeps trying
to spit out
of its throat.

Take cover!
Aki-*sensei* shouts.

We grab on to
walls,
grab on to
each other,
grab on to
anything
to stay
upright.

IF THE QUAKES CONTINUE,

the sea could
rise up again,
take what's left—
can't let that happen.

I'm going out! I shout.

Wait, Aki-*sensei* says.
The earth's
still shaking.

Principal Kunihara
won't let anyone
out of sight.

I don't care.
The earth's not waiting!
Why should I?

THE SHAKING STOPS

and I breathe again,
relieved.
It's just a 7.1—
not like the first one,
the 9.0
that lifted doors
and walls
and the ocean
floor.

HANDS AND FEET NUMB,

we curl up
on the hardwood
floor
and wait.

Ganbarimasu—
Together, we'll endure.

Principal Kunihara carries boxes
under his arm.
What for?

He says we'll tear the cardboard
to make signs.

We use what we have.

I write in marker
salvaged from the
art room—

LOOKING FOR MY GRANDPARENTS:
HIROYUKI AND SANAE TAKAMOTO.
HAS ANYONE SEEN
TOMOKO TAKAMOTO?

Tape the signs
to the auditorium wall.

WE SECTION OFF

sleeping spaces
with cardboard,
tarps,
blankets,
tents,
lines of tape
drawn
across the floor.

All we've got
are old futons
and blankets so short
my feet stick out
from under them.

It will be a cold night
in the auditorium.

I try to close my eyes.
Try not to think
about Mom,

about *Ojiichan*
and *Obaachan,*
about all my friends.

Try to focus on
this other tide,
the one inside me—
Me.
Kai.
Still alive.

Amidst

IN MY DREAMS

I play soccer
with my friends,
like I used to do
so long ago.

But we're trapped—
Shin, Ryu, and I
can't kick the ball
through a wall of water
even Kagawa* or Honda†
couldn't penetrate.

---

* Shinji Kagawa—(b. 1989) Plays midfield for the German club
  Borussia Dortmund and for the Japan national team Soccer Nippon
  Daihyō

† Keisuke Honda—(b. 1986) Plays midfield or forward for the Italian club
  AC Milan and for the Japan national team Soccer Nippon Daihyō

WIND BLOWS THE DOORS OPEN

in the middle of the night,
batters them shut again.
I bolt upright, panicked.

Is it me,
or is the earth
still moving?

A snowstorm's arrived
and it's pitch-black outside
but I don't care—
I'm getting out of here.

TIPTOEING LIKE A NINJA

I feel my way
around the room,
stepping over boxes,
shoes, people.

I'm almost at the door
when Taro Nishi
jumps up
in front of me.

Where do you think
you're going?
he asks.
Where does it look like?
I say, pushing my classmate aside.

But he blocks my
path,
like he always
does.

Move!
I say,
shoving him
out of the way.

What's your problem?
Taro snarls.

My problem?
How about
no water
no food
no electricity
no heat
no family

no future?
Gotta find my mom!

Rescue teams are
doing their best,
he says,
holding me back.

If your mom's out there,
they'll find her.

I struggle against
his grip,
try to break free.
What if they don't?

He doesn't have an answer,
so I go slack
in his arms,
then squat when he
relaxes his grip.
I kick him
backward in the shins,
ram my body into his,
break away,
rush for the door.

I've got nothing
left to lose.

AKI-*SENSEI* RUNS OVER,

grabs me tightly,
whirls me around
to face him
in the darkness.

We've got to keep our heads,
he says, jutting his chin
toward the scuffed
floor
where kids
huddle together
in the dark,
wide-eyed,
scared.

BACK IN MY CORNER

I pound my fists
into my futon,
rage like the sea.

Next to me,
old folks
burrow into their
blankets,
murmur:
It's just like the war,*
when we had
nothing.

Obaachan used to talk about
how hard things were
back then,

when a banana
was a luxury,
green tea was
champagne.

She told me all this
so I'd appreciate
what I had.

But I didn't.
Until now.

....

* Refers to Second World War

At daybreak
sun streams through
mud-streaked windows.

In the hallway mirror
I see my seaweed hair,
dirt-smudged face,
bloodshot brown eyes.

Sliding paste
over my teeth
with my fingers,
seawater still
on my tongue.

Can't get the mud
out from under my nails—
my skin, my hair.
Must be how Mom felt
washing my dirty soccer clothes.

The cold water turns brown,
brown like my
first soccer uniform—
my very own team jersey
shining like
a stallion.

Sharp white stripes
running like arrows
down the sides.

Ryu said
kakko ii
—cool—
and I felt that way.

Ryu!
I haven't seen him
since the bridge.

LOOKING UP

from the sink—
a face
behind mine
in the mirror.

Can it be?
Buzz-cut hair
like a monk's,
eyes slit-sharp
like a lizard's.

What?
Shin!
No way!
You're here!

Kai! Hey!
You made it!
We made it!
Oi! Oi! he says,
laughing.
We slap
each other's backs.

Never thought
I'd be so
happy again.

My dad and mom
are here, too,
and my grandpa!
he says, taking
me by the arm.

But I don't
move.
Oh,

he says.
Oh.

THEN WE SEE

Keiko Inoue—
the coach's daughter,
scratched, bruised,
bandaged
but alive.

She blushes,
as if embarrassed
at being seen
without clean clothes
or brushed hair,
and even more
embarrassed
about being
embarrassed
at a time like this.

Last time I saw you,
you were under a desk,
I blurt out.

Despite ourselves,
we both laugh.

I'm glad you're okay,
she says.

Me too.
I mean, you too, I reply.
Suddenly I forget where I am,
why we're here.

ONIGIRI! *

someone shouts.

Five rice balls
for every twenty people
and hot green tea.

Won't even make a dent
in my grumbling stomach,
but I'm still
grateful.

....

* *onigiri*—riceball

Shin's *ojiisan**
waves his *onigiri* away,
holds it out
to Shin instead.

Shin shakes his head.
You gotta eat, Grandpa, he says.
After all you've been through,
what a waste it would be
to die this way.

We all heard of the man who froze
last night in a shelter
rather than take the last blanket.

Shin puts the *onigiri* into
his grandfather's mouth
like feeding a baby bird.

Shin's father looks so old—
not like he did behind the wheel of his taxi,
straight-backed and proud.

....

*   *ojiisan*—a more formal way to say "grandfather," usually describing
     someone else's

His hair turned gray
overnight.

Shin's *ojiisan* held on to
the washing machine hose
on their balcony
for eighteen hours
while the water
whirled and churned
around him
and the air turned
to ice.

Their apartment's gone—
now just chunks
of sludge-covered
concrete.

Their family fleet of taxis,
vanished.
Everything's gone.

Well, not everything—
they still have
each other.

THE RADIO TELLS OF WHOLE VILLAGES

wiped out
along the Tohoku coast—
Rikuzentakata,
Minamisanriku,
Ishinomaki,
Onagawa,
Kesennuma.

Tens of thousands
could be dead or injured,
thousands more missing,
hundreds of thousands
homeless,
including me.

The prime minister
says we're not alone.

I feel alone.

Can't stop checking
my ruined
phone.

Principal Kunihara says
they'll try
to find my dad
in New York.

Good luck with that.
Haven't seen him
in six years—
like he's really
gonna come back
to a disaster zone.

AFTER THE PRINCIPAL LEAVES,

I whisper to Keiko:
I'm getting out of here.

Don't, she says,
her small body tensing.
It's not safe.

I don't care, I say.

What could possibly hurt me
more than this quake
already has?

I tell her the story
I heard
about the guy
a town away
who scuba dived
into the tsunami
to rescue his wife.

And when
his wife was safe
he went *back*
into the wave
to get his
mother-in-law.

*Going out now is nothing
compared to that!*

You're crazy, she says,
but I swear I see her smile.

I'M ABOUT TO MAKE A BREAK FOR IT

when Aki-*sensei*
comes toward us,
that look on his face.

10 9 8 7 6 5 4 3 2 1

I count my breaths,
ticking off
the seconds
like Ryu and I used to do
at the end
of a soccer game,
trading glances
when there was still
a chance to win.

Go away,
I say to myself,
willing him
to turn around.

Please just
go away.

HE PUTS HIS ARM AROUND ME,

says *Obaachan*'s body
has washed
ashore.

I'm sorry.
I'm afraid
you will have to identify her,
he says formally,
head bowed low.

Identify her?
I repeat.

Yes. He nods,
sighs the saddest sigh.
To confirm.
Do you think
you can do that?

I blink back tears.
Confirm.
How can I confirm?
I guess so,
I reply.
But really,
I have no idea.

No idea
at all.

PULLING MY HOOD UP OVER MY HEAD,

I finally go outside,
now the last place
I want to be.

Aki-*sensei* and I walk slowly
through the darkened town.

Shock of cold air,
shock of
muddy wreckage
piled high
as Mount Fuji.

Streets clogged
with wooden beams
like broken ghost ships,
shattered shells of houses
floating in oil slicks.

Fire smell.
Ocean smell.
Death smell
that doesn't go away

even when I tie a cloth
over my nose
and mouth.

Passing the elementary school,
my brain doesn't want
to do the math—

74 out of 108
10 out of 13

What percent is that?

That's how many
students and teachers
we lost.

At the edge of town
the fish-processing factory's
a makeshift morgue.

People laid out
on slabs of wood
on metal tables
inside the open room.

I squint when we find
Obaachan,
as if taking in
only half the picture
will make it hurt
half as much.

OBAACHAN'S SWEATER—

mud-soaked,
brown—
I see faint
pink and purple stripes
on the hand-knit
weave.
I
know
it's her.

AT LEAST

I'll be able to
console her spirit,
chant prayers,
light incense,

make offerings,
like the braised pumpkin
Obaachan
loved so much.

At least the priest and I
can dress her body
in a white paper kimono,
which will burn
down to ash
in the flames.

At least
I can say
good-bye.

OBAACHAN AND *OJIICHAN*

always did
everything
together—

what if
they find
him next?

Back at the shelter
I'm terrified
of getting
more news.

SHIN, KEIKO, AND I KEEP BUSY

sorting donated supplies—
blankets, food,
water, towels, tea.

Heavy box in his hands,
Shin stops,
cocks his head,
says—
Wait! Stop! Hold on!

I look at him, puzzled.
Then the earth rumbles
and I drop the box I'm holding.
Shin and Keiko
drop their boxes, too—
we're pitched sideways.

Everything we've just
spent hours packing
spills out.

WHOA! I THINK I FELT THAT BEFORE IT HAPPENED!

Shin says, righting himself.
I can tell he's spooked—
not as much as I am.

Some people can hear a sound wave
before a quake, he says,
packing up the boxes again.
Usually there's too much noise
to really listen.

We've had quakes before,
but he's never told me this.

I guess I have dog ears, Shin says,
adding that he felt weird
the morning the quake hit,
like he was wearing shoes
on the wrong feet.

I didn't notice anything.
I wish I had.
I wish I could have

done something,
anything.

Shin says quakes send out vibrations
that move through the ground like waves,
traveling ten times the speed of sound.

Dogs, birds, insects,
even spiders
can sometimes feel them.

Some animals
feel a quake coming,
flee to higher ground.

Wish I'd listened harder, Shin says.

LATER WE TRUDGE UP THE HILL

behind the school,
past the rice paddies
near the shrine,
taking bottled water,
onigiri, mikan,*

....

* *mikan*—Japanese tangerines

toilet paper,
magazines,
cans of green tea,
bags of *senbei**
to the old folks
who can't
come down.

BOWING LOW

the people
stand outside their homes,
happy the world
hasn't forgotten them.

But some feel guilty
that their homes
are still standing—
say they feel terrible
that they survived.

I don't say anything,

but I know
how they feel.

* *senbei*—rice crackers

Even though my pack's now empty,
my shoulders are weighted down.

SEE THIS? SHIN ASKS,

crouching
at the ancient stone marker
beside the mountain road:

Don't build beneath this stone.

1,200 years ago
another tsunami came
and washed away
the village.

Must have walked by this sign
a hundred times—
how did we miss it?

Back in ancient Greece
Thucydides watched
a giant wave wash over his town
after a quake, Shin says—
the quake caused the wave.

Like when you drop a stone into
a bowl of water
it sprays over the sides.

Doesn't take someone
like Thucydides
to figure it out.

He's mad.
I've never seen him so mad.
Like he somehow blames himself.
I blame myself, too,
but that won't change
what happened.
Nothing will.

IN THE HOSPITAL PARKING LOT—

rows of photos
laid out on blue tarps.

Caked in mud,
streaked with sludge,
warped from water.

I search for pictures
of Mom

so I can show people,
ask, *Have you seen her?*

Find instead
a single torn image
of Mom and Dad
sitting cross-legged
on the tatami mat in our living room.

He's wearing a striped green flannel shirt
and jeans—
cigarette in one hand,
guitar in the other.
She's in a red floral dress,
her long straight hair
held back with a paisley headband.
She's leaning gently into him.
He's holding on to me.

Once,
a long
time ago,
we were together.

A happy family.

DAD HAD ROUND GLASSES

like John Lennon,
wanted to play
in a band.
Mom had ruddy
red cheeks, ebony eyes.
Maybe he thought
she was his
Yoko Ono.
Maybe they thought:
All you need is love.

I STILL REMEMBER

Dad strumming his guitar
until his finger joints locked
or he busted a string—
whichever came first.

He was always trying to see
how far he could stretch.

Talking too much, singing to himself
as he walked along the pier,

laughing loudly—
things a Japanese dad
would never do.

He embarrassed me so bad,
sometimes I wished
he'd go away.
And then,
one day,
he did.

DIDN'T EVEN KNOW

Mom had such a photo.

I kneel down to pick it up,
put it in my jacket pocket.
I don't tell anyone,
not even Shin.

DON'T NEED DOG EARS

to hear the five o'clock chime
ring out from the PA system
across town.

I turn left and walk
a beeline—
like I've done
for years.

Where are you going? Shin asks,
turning right instead.

I've turned toward home.

FOR SEVENTEEN YEARS

that chime meant
time to go home,
time for dinner.

*Why don't they
turn that thing off?* I shout.

Yeah, they should, Shin says, frowning.

*Why do you care?
You've still got your family!*
As soon as I say it,
I regret it.

But like so much else,
it's already too late.

Sorry!
Shin says,
but I'm off and running.

I hear him coming
up fast behind me,
whirl around.

Don't follow me! I say,
but my words are swallowed
by the whirl of a helicopter overhead.

News team?
Rescue crews scouring the land
for signs of life?
Go away!
I say, running into
the wind.

RAIN BEATS DOWN,

and wild-eyed dogs and cats
don't even run for cover.

A dog trails me,
begging for food.

I shoo it away,
like I pushed
Shin away.

Even though
Shin's my best friend,
he doesn't understand.

People who didn't
lose anyone
can't really
understand.

I NEED TO GO BACK HOME,

even if home
is no longer there.

Have to see
for myself.

Have to know.
Have to
go.

THE SUZUKIS' YELLOW HOUSE

stands in front of me
like a beacon—

the only house
left on my street.

Half sunk into the ground,
windows blown out,

covered in slime.

Big red X on the door.

Someone didn't make it.

WARPED SKELETON,

sheetrock trash heap,
crumpled wood,
chunks of stone.

This used to be my home?

Now I can't even
call it a house.

Down on my knees,
clawing through
oily slime
bare-handed.

Where is everything?
Nothing left.

WHERE ARE THE WISHES

I wrote
on strips of colored paper
for the *Tanabata* festival*
so many years ago?

Every year
the same thing:
I want to be a
soccer player.

After he left,
too proud to write:

....

* *Tanabata* festival—a festival celebrating the meeting of the deities
Orihime and Hikoboshi (the stars Vega and Altair), who legend holds
are separated by the Milky Way. Tanabata falls on either July 7 or
August 7, depending on region. On this day, people write their wishes
for the year on strips of paper and hang them on bamboo trees.

Wish Dad
would come
back home.

WONDER WHERE

Dad is now.
Hasn't been in touch
for years.

Is he still in New York?
Or is he
up on some
mountaintop
meditating,
cut off from
everything—
the last person
in the world
to know what's
happened here.

Otherwise
he'd try
to find
me.

Wouldn't he?

Can't believe
he wouldn't
get in touch
after all
that's happened—
after all
the unbelievable things
that have happened.

Has he even tried?

How can I think of Dad
when Mom's not here?

I kick myself.

She's the one
who stayed,
after all.

IN THE RUBBLE

all I find is a ceramic rice bowl,
fired in a kiln so hot

even the flames
that ate our town
after the sea
swept through it
couldn't destroy it.

Ashore

TWO WEEKS AFTER THE TSUNAMI

our school reopens
so we can graduate.*

Strange to walk
these broken halls,
strange to sit
on the chairs we used
to tilt back
on two legs,
defying gravity,
to see if we could fly.

Notebooks, pencils, erasers,
paper, ballpoint pens
donated by the truckful.

But it's hard to focus
with bulldozers

* In the Japanese school calendar, graduation is held at the end of March.

eating up
what's left.
outside.

All I can do
is write down
what I've seen
for Mom
when she
comes back.

BASEBALL PLAYERS, MODELS, MOVIE STARS

come to cheer us up.
Laughter sounds
like a foreign language here.

Volunteers arrive
by the busload,
sleep in cars and tents,
eager to help out.

People from all over the world
put on waterproof jackets,
pants, boots, gloves,
helmets, goggles, and face masks,

walk through town
like lost snowboarders.

Side by side, foreigners and Japanese,
clear drains,
wash away mud,
haul trash,
pick through
collapsed
houses.

At the canning factory,
they shovel
octopus and salmon
squid and mackerel
into burlap bags,
carry them to the shoreline,
return the dead fish
to the sea.

The emperor and empress
fly in, too—
and a bearded man
in a sweet potato truck
wearing a long black coat

and a wide-brimmed hat,
like someone from
another world.

Keiko rushes to the door.
Who or what is that? I ask.
The rabbi smiles,
shakes my hand,
explains his attire,
passes out the food.

Some people cry with joy
at such a simple thing—
a hot meal.
Sweet potatoes!
Natsukashii . . .*

I tell Keiko that
I'm happy, too,
happy for the
distraction.

....

*   *natsukashii*—expression of a feeling of nostalgia or fondness when
    experiencing something for the first time in a long time

Keiko nods, listening.
She doesn't have to say it,
but I know she feels the same way.

They haven't found
her dad yet, either.

ON GRADUATION DAY

Principal Kunihara hands out
our diplomas
in the makeshift
classroom.

Yoku ganbarimashita, he says—
you did your best—
holding the papers
between trembling hands,
bowing low to each of us.

His hands shake.
His voice shakes.
He doesn't even try
to stop the tears,
though half the room
is full of TV crews

where half the class
should have been.

SHIN'S FAMILY

stands quietly
by my side.

Shin's dad, mom, and grandpa
congratulate me.
I fight back tears.
Ryu's not here.
Mom's not here.
Ojiichan and *Obaachan*
are not here.
Dad's . . . *wherever.*

Is this my
family
now?

PEOPLE TALK ABOUT

getting back
to normal.

Can we ever
be *normal*
again?

NOTHING IS NORMAL

when out of the blue
Old Man Sato
comes to sit by my side,
his short white hair
sticking up like quills,
his knees almost
touching mine.

He tells me how
Ojiichan and *Obaachan* met
at fourteen,
went to high school together,
married after
graduation,
then had my mom,
their only child.

Ojiichan lived here all his life,
proud to carry on
the family tradition

as his father had done
before him.

Old Man Sato is
a fisherman, too,
netting silver-gray mackerel.
He swallows,
brushes away a tear, tells me
he saw *Ojiichan*
get into his boat,
rush into the ocean
to beat the wave
just after the quake hit.

Old Man Sato says he's sorry,
but he couldn't bring himself
to tell me
until after graduation,
until now.

He rode into the tsunami?
Why? I ask.
It sounds so crazy.

That's what we've done
for hundreds of years.

He did the right thing.
He did what any good fisherman
would have done.

In what might have been
his last moments,
he thought of the future.

The closer a tsunami gets to land,
the higher and stronger it grows.

Ojiichan wanted
to save his boat,
the one his father
had taught him
how to build
with his own
two hands.

For you, Old Man Sato says.
For me? I ask.

If he went far enough
into the surf,
he'd escape the crash
of the waves.

Old Man Sato's obsidian
eyes glisten.

They found
pieces of Grandpa's boat
crushed like seashells
against the rocky
shore.

WASN'T THAT THE SAME BOAT

Mom and I rode in?
Just like the one from
Pirates of the Caribbean
at Disneyland—

when we screamed and laughed,
careened into dark tunnels,
ducked fireballs from muskets.
Wasn't that the same boat
we rode calmly on the waves,
going farther out
to where Grandpa lowered his nets
and pulled up his silvery mackerel?

The boat's now gone.
Ojiichan's now gone.

That ocean—
the one I used to love—
is gone.

WHAT'S LEFT IS JUST A MEMORY

and a mass of junk—
that's what it looks like,
covered in mud and oil.

UNTIL THE DAY

Shin sees something
peering out
from a pile
we're clearing
near the school.

Muddy,
slimy,
not quite round—
but still
its black
and white
checks are
unmistakable . . .

a soccer ball.

Shin lifts it with his toes,
taps it lightly,
kicks it over to me.

Wet and soggy,
the ball bumps off his foot,
thuds toward me
on the ground.

No, I say, kick it away
with the top of my foot
as if it were an animal
that might bite.

But I can't help noticing
the way my leg moved
as if it had a mind
of its own—
how good it felt
to touch a ball
again.
Gotta push that feeling down.
Don't want to think about
those times
again.

DON'T NOTICE

the little boy watching us
from the auditorium window,
face pressed against the glass,
fogging it up.

Now he's outside,
arms crossed
over his chest.
*Can you teach
me how to play?*
he asks.

Sorry, I say.
Not now.
He frowns, digs his toes
into the mud.
*You guys are playing.
It's not fair!*

*We shouldn't be out here
playing, either,*
Shin says.

But you are!

It's one thing
to take our minds off
what's happened—
but with so many people hurting,
having a good time
doesn't feel right.

Just once! he begs,
pulling on my sleeve.

What if you get hurt?
The hospital doesn't need
more patients.

I won't get hurt! he says.

He's got jagged black bangs
and he's stubborn—
like Ryu.

He reminds me of myself,
too—
how tough I was
when my father went
back to New York,
and I had

to be
the man.

Ask me later, I say,
hoping he'll
forget.

A FEW DAYS LATER

he pushes a box
toward my corner.

Here, he says,
tilting his chin up.
Open it.

I look inside,
find small oval discs,
elastic bands.

What's this?

We made them out of tires.
He picks one up,
puts it on his leg.
Shin protectors.

I look at him sideways.
Why did you make these? I ask.

You said we'd get hurt.
Now we won't get hurt.

Oh great, I think.
A real smart one.

Will you play with us now?
He smiles,
knowing he's won.

My friends call me Guts, he says.

Just this once, I say.
But don't tell anyone!

YES!
....

Guts high-fives me.

Come on, everyone!
he shouts.

I told you not to tell anyone!
I say.

Sorryyyy, he says,
grinning,
as he hands out the protectors
to his friends.

TATTERED BALL UNDER MY ARM,

I signal to Shin to
follow us out.

We walk up the hill
to the empty field,
send the kids jogging
in circles,
then lead
them in stretches.

The ball is almost flat
and not nearly as good
as the one I used to have.
Wonder where it
is now.

They take turns
with the mushy ball,
dribbling,

passing,
running,
shouting.

Guts kicks it hard,
whoops when it
somehow
gets off the ground.

He doesn't know
which part of the foot
to kick with,
but it doesn't matter.

It's the first time
he's smiled
in weeks.

WHEN I WAS HIS AGE,

I'd wake up every morning
at six to jog
and juggle.

Right leg,
left leg,
alternating right and left,

thighs,
head,
mixed.

I wasn't
very good,
and everyone teased me
for trying.
They teased me, too,
because I looked
like Dad—*Hafu.**

Ojiichan said that I was "Double,"†
not *Hafu*—
had the best
of both worlds.

He said
to ignore what
the mean kids said.

....

* *Hafu*—somebody who is half Japanese. The word *Hafu* comes from
the English word *half*, indicating half Japanese, half foreign. The label
first became popular in the 1970s, but many consider it diminishing.

† Double—term coined in the early 2000s as an alternative to *Hafu* to
describe biracial kids, emphasizing the "double good" of being from
two cultures

Teased *and* bullied . . .
don't think that's
the *Double*
he had in mind.

I kept at it anyway,
and when I juggled to twenty,
Ojiichan took me inland
to a Vegalta Sendai game
so I could see the pros play.

High up in the stands,
we cheered and waved flags,
jumping up with each goal.

I got a bright yellow T-shirt,
wore it until
it was so thin
you could see through it.

FROM THEN ON

I spent my Saturdays
practicing in the dust
and dirt
until my white socks
were brown,

until I had the ball
right where
I wanted it.
I could juggle a hundred times
straight,
could finally
try out
for the team.

I THOUGHT THINGS WOULD GET BETTER

once I made the team,
but they didn't.

My teammates
never passed to me.
They stole my ball.
They spit on me
and kicked me, hard,
trying to make me
go away.

Coach Inoue told us
we were a team,
and a team
should play together.

I WAS MIDFIELDER—

in the middle,
where I'd been
all my life.

Between Mom and Dad,
Japan and America,
ocean and land.

My dream
of playing soccer
was all I had,
so I chased it
and chased it
and chased it.

No matter what happened,
I wouldn't go away.

Dad always said
we weren't quitters,
and I wanted
to be like him.

Even the forward,
Taro Nishi—

who teased me the most—
had to get over it.

After all,
he needed my assists
to score.

SOME FAMOUS JAPANESE PLAYERS

played for foreign teams,
Dad said.

If you speak English,
you can be like them—
try out for any soccer club
in the world.

The world
is your oyster,
Mom said,
laughing
at her own cliché.

She knew I hated
the slimy things
she sometimes

brought home
from work,
would only eat them
occasionally,
and only then
if they were *kaki furai**—
never, ever
raw.

I DIDN'T HAVE CLOSE FRIENDS—

most of my classmates
hung out at the rec center,
their thumbs dancing
over Game Boys,
heads buried in manga
thick as telephone books.

Then Shin joined the team.
After him came Ryu.
Like me,
they lived for soccer,
each for his own reasons.

*   *kaki furai*—breaded, deep-fried oysters

Shin was weak
from a childhood illness
and wanted to be strong.
He played defense
and always made me laugh
with his jokes.
He never gave up
even when his legs
wobbled.

Goalkeeper Ryu
was tall as a giant,
though he wanted
to be smaller
to fit in at school.
He was fast and fearless,
could send the ball
all the way to Mars.
Someday he wanted to play
for Samurai Blue.

I trained hard because I wanted
to make Dad proud,
to make him stay.

MOM AND DAD CHEERED ME ON

from the sidelines,
brought *onigiri* and tea,
carried buckets of ice to
dip our towels into
when it was hot and humid.

After games,
they took me out
for ramen,
tried not to argue,
said they loved me
even when we lost.

ONE DAY DAD WENT TO THE PINE FOREST

to play guitar
and sing.

But he didn't
come back.

At first I didn't worry—
Mom said
he'd be back.

He sometimes stayed
for hours,
but he always
came back.

He'll be back
soon,
Obaachan assured us—
he always
comes back.

WE KEPT ON

when snow frosted
the pine needles in winter
and cherry blossom petals
fell to the streets in spring
and fireworks bloomed like flowers
over the hilltop in summer
and Mom's oysters came up for harvest
and *Ojiichan* took his boat
out for mackerel
in autumn.

But season
after season

Dad didn't
come
back.

MY WORLD BECAME ONE SMALL BALL—

I could
make it
spin at will.
I could toss it
into the air.
I could
catch it
midflight,
kick it
to the stars,
block it
with my body,
make it
fly.

I poured all
my hope
into that
ball—
a tiny

globe
between my
feet—
the one thing
I could
always make
come
back.

I DREAMED OF HEARING DAD

on the radio,
imagined telling Shin and Ryu,
That's my dad,
turning up the volume loud.

But I never heard his voice
across the airwaves
or anywhere at all.

All I heard was
Mom,
singing in the shower:
If you love someone,
set them
free.

IT HURT TOO MUCH TO HOPE,

so after a while
I buried
the parts of me
that were like him.

When Mom spoke to me
in English,
I answered back
in Japanese.

I wore hats to hide
my light-brown hair.

I put away
my soccer ball,
and with it
all my dreams.

夏

Summer

Astray

IT'S BEEN FORTY-NINE DAYS

since
the tsunami
swept through our town.

Forty-nine days—
that's how long
it takes the souls
of the departed
to leave this world.

I haven't given up hope
that Mom
will come back,
that Ryu's still
out there,
somewhere.

But we need
to send
the spirits off. . . .

I CARRY A RED SNAPPER

in both hands
as Shin and I walk
through the forest
up to the shrine
to pay our respects.

How did Keiko get it?
Someone must have
brought it to her
at the shelter.

Now Shin and I bring it
up the mountain—
Keiko's become a *hikikomori**
and won't go out.

We place my grandpa's favorite fish
on the altar,
and everyone laughs.
Even on such a solemn occasion,
Keiko's made us smile.

* *hikikomori*—a shut-in, someone who refuses to leave home

I offer Mom
green tea KitKats.
I bring a glass of Nikka whiskey
for *Ojiichan,*
adzuki bean mochi and
stewed pumpkin
for *Obaachan.*

Foods I once
took for granted,
now a feast.

We put *Obaachan*'s ashes
into the earth
and I say good-bye.

DOWN BY THE BROKEN BRIDGE

we make origami boats,
float them out
on the river

to
send our loved ones' spirits
safely

to
the other
side.

SAFE TRAVELS,

Mom, Ojiichan,
Obaachan.

At least
you're up
there
in heaven
together.
I'm down
here
on Earth

alone.

MY LITTLE BOAT

drifts
aimlessly,

like the days
that go by

without word
from Dad.

I FINALLY GIVE IN

and play soccer
with Guts, but only
because he asks me
for the thousandth time,
just won't take *no*
for an answer.

I'M PLAYING SOCCER WITH GUTS

and his friends
when Taro storms up,
face as red as a *tengu** spirit.

*How can you be out here
having fun
when people are suffering?*
he shouts, arms flailing.

....

* *tengu*—Japanese mythological being, usually a human and avian
mixture depicted with a red face and a very long nose

The kids trip
over themselves
to get away.

Stupid foreigner, he spits.
Never were
a team player!

IN A SECOND

I'm on top of him,
and we're rolling
on each other
like wild dogs,
tearing
at each other's
ill-fitting
donated
clothes.

Shin's dad
jumps in,
pulls us apart.

We know you're
under stress,
but you have

to set an example,
he says.

I don't want
to be
an example!
I shout.

Haven't I
been through enough
already?

Taro breaks away,
runs off,
panting.

What happened?
Shin's dad asks.

I shake my head.
I don't know.
Taro's always had it
in for me.

Shin's father shoots me
a sideways look.
Really?

I swear!

Okay. Try to calm down.
He puts a hand
on my shoulder
almost as quickly
as I flick it off.

I'm shaking.
My lip trembles.
I try not to cry.

Let it out,
Shin's dad says softly.

I shake my head no.
I can't.

You have to, he says.
What you hold in
will eat you up.

Then let it eat me, I say.
Let me feed the monster.
Let it have a feast.

You'll make yourself sick,
he says.

Good! I shout.
Then maybe
I'll just
die.

The palm of his hand
finds my cheek,
hard.

It stings
so bad.

I'm shaking
all over.

You want to know what I feel?
I shout.
I hate myself.
Okay?
I hate you
and this town
and everyone here!

Shin's father puts his
hands across his heart,
as if each word
is a body blow.

Well, what did he expect?
He's the one
who hit me,
said, "Let it out."

I'm sorry, I didn't mean to . . .
he says, upset.

Go away! I shout.

Kai . . . , Shin's dad says, softly.
The way my mom
used to say it.

Kai.
It means ocean.
Mom named me that
to anchor me.

GO *AWAY!*

I RUN UP THE HILL TO THE MOUNTAINS,

the place Dad always went.

Why do I end up
hurting everyone
I care about,
and why does it
hurt me most?

I try to remember
calming breaths
Coach Inoue taught me,
but even those
are gone.

I NEVER SHOULD HAVE

touched that soccer ball,
never should have played with Guts,
never should have
let my body remember
what I'd tried
so hard
to forget:

The day a brand-new soccer ball
arrived from America
after my dad
had been gone a year.
How excited I was
that he'd finally
remembered me.

But then a photo of Dad
fluttered out—
Was that his new wife?
It was clear
he'd replaced
his old dreams—
no more room
for me.

I GUESS I COULD TRY TO TRACK HIM DOWN.

A couple of years ago,
I found him once on Facebook—
at least I think it was him.
I didn't have the nerve to make
a friend request.
What if he ignored it?

What if he said no?
Couldn't do it.

NIGHT FALLS,

and I realize
I've been gone
for hours.

When I go back to the shelter,
Keiko rushes up
talking a mile a minute
about some guy named Kenji
who came to see me.

I don't want to see him, I mumble.
Whoever he is.

Yes you do!

No I don't!

*It's the tenth anniversary of
9/11 . . .*

What's that got to do with me?

I stop, think—
New York. Dad.

Then she says in English,
You'd be with
other orphans.

What? I blink.
Other islands? Huh?

Orphans.

I'm not
an orphan!

It's the first time
I've heard the word
applied to me,
and I want
to rip
it off.

KEIKO LOOKS STRAIGHT AT ME,

unlike most girls,
who look away.

My anger
doesn't scare her,
and that makes
my anger small.

Are you *going?* I ask.
I'm not going anywhere,
she says, stomps her foot
on the wooden floor.

That way, Dad will know
where to find me
when he comes back.

Oh, I sigh.

You have to go
for both of us,
she says.

I WISH

I could,
wish I was the person
Keiko thinks I am,
but I'm just not
strong enough.

I shake my head.

Keiko's eyes
turn to glass,
like they did
that day in March.

She thinks I'm a loser.
She's right.

Fine! she says, storming off.
Be that way!

Taro Nishi shoots me a look
from the corner,
where he's pretending to read a newspaper.
And then he smiles.

I want to smash his face in.
Shin tries to calm me down.
I want to push him away, too.
He's my best friend!
What's wrong with me?

That's when I know
I can't stay here anymore,
pretending Shin's family
is my family,
wishing everything
was okay.

EVERYONE'S WISHING THESE DAYS—

strips of colored paper
hang from bamboo stalks
for Tanabata,
the one time of year
two star-crossed lovers can
meet in the sky.

It's the one time each year
wishes might actually
have a chance to come true—

but for the first time ever,
I have no wish.

THE LITTLE KIDS HAVE LOTS OF WISHES.

Keiko gathers them around,
tells them of the legend,
tries to give them hope.

*Princess Orihime wove her beautiful cloth
by the banks of the Milky Way.
Her father, the Sky King,
loved her art.
She worked hard to please him,*
Keiko says.

*Hikoboshi, a cowherd,
lived on the other side
of the river.*

*They fell in love
and married.*

*They were so happy
that Orihime forgot all about her weaving*

and Hikoboshi let his cows
roam wild.

The Sky King got mad,
separated them
on opposite riverbanks.

Orihime begged the king
to let them meet again.

I jump into the story,
act like the Sky King,
put on a scary face.

The king agreed,
but only for one day a year—
the seventh day
of the seventh month—
and only if his daughter
finished her weaving, I say.

The kids' eyes are wide, waiting.
Keiko and I take turns.

Orihime kept her promise,
but when the two tried to meet,

they couldn't cross the river—
the bridge was gone, she says.

A flock of magpies
heard Orihime's cries,
made a bridge with their wings,
I jump in.

Keiko says,
But if it rains on Tanabata,
the magpies won't fly,
won't fight against
the water.

The last words are mine:
And the princess
and her cowherd
have to wait another year.

WHAT ARE YOU GOING TO WISH FOR?

I ask the kids.
I'm going to wish
for Tanabata,
Guts says.

At first I think
he's being clever,
but then
I understand.

Tanabata won't come
if it rains.
Ever since the tsunami,
the weather
has been strange—
like the Earth
doesn't know
what season
we're in.

Pray for clear skies tomorrow,
Keiko says,
steepling her fingers together
at her heart.

The kids close their eyes,
faces pinched
in concentration,
wishing.

I start praying, too.
These kids
can't afford
to have their wishes
rained away.

HOW WILL THE COWHERD
AND HIS WEAVER MEET

on Tanabata
if the bridge
is gone?

There's no more bridge
across the skies.

No more bridge
across the river
where Dad first taught me
how to swim.

No more bridge
across the river
where Shin, Ryu, and I
used to catch crayfish
and skateboard.

Everything
between the river
and the coast
is gone.

RYU WAS STRONGER

than Shin
and me
put together,
and now
he's gone,
too.

Remembering Ryu,
I pray some more.

IT DOES NOT RAIN ON TANABATA—

seems like Orihime
and Hikoboshi
and all the other people
we've lost
are looking down
from heaven,
praying for *us*.

MY TANABATA WISH ALWAYS HUNG

on my bulletin board,
next to Dad's:
I want to be a soccer player.

I don't want to be
a soccer player anymore.

Don't think
I'll ever see
Dad again.

Don't know
if Mom's
ever
coming back.

Just want to leave
this place
like they did.

So I make my plan.

Aloft

I SHOVE CLOTHES INTO MY PACK,

grab water and food,
wait for my chance.

It arrives the day
a comedian comes
to make *soba**
and everyone crowds
around the pots,
enjoying themselves
so much
that no one notices
me slipping away.

---

*   *soba*—buckwheat noodles

RUNNING THROUGH MY RUINED TOWN,

pack flapping
winglike
against my back.

Plowing through blocks
strewn with heaps of
refrigeratorsblackboardsbicyclestaxis
bustedpianosshelvesdesksstairs
allmixedtogether
in a marshland
grave,
waiting to be taken away.

Down by the ocean
I pass the park
where twisted swing sets creak,
moving with the wind.

I run along the broken seawall
where we'd planned
to skateboard
that day the sea
stormed up
to land.

I jog along the coastline
where black pines once
crowded the edges—
now just one remains.

I keep running
and don't look back.
Can't look back.

IN A NEIGHBORING TOWN

I sit at the beach
in the midday sun,
catch my breath
amidst the ruins.

The log
next to mine
starts to move.

Huh? I jump up,
heart racing.

What the . . . ?

It's a man,
covered in sand.

I tap him softly
with my foot.

He lifts his head,
squints against
the sun.

Are you okay? I ask.

I'm not dead.
Just drunk,
he croaks.

That's good, I say, relieved.

Drunk is good? he asks.
I laugh.

Combing his hands
through the sand,
he takes a beer
from a buried six-pack,
hands it to me.

My first beer—
Mom wouldn't approve, I know.

But I smile
and raise the can
to say *kanpai.**

I'm toasting
Ojiichan—
it's his favorite
brand.

My wife and baby died,
the man says,
voice dry
and cracked.

That's horrible.
I spit the warm beer
out of my mouth.

Yeah. He laughs
darkly.

Why is he laughing?
I want to ask.

....

* *kanpai*—cheers; a toast

137

But he catches my startled expression,
reads my mind.

I'm laughing to thank you
for not saying
I'm sorry.

My son had just been born.
I had to register his birth
and his death
on the same day.

And the worst thing?
I wasn't the only one.

He looks at me,
then out to the sea,
pops open
another can.

We sip together,
listen to the waves
for the longest time.
I think my mom's dead, too, I say.
He nods, sighs, then sighs again.

I TELL HIM ABOUT RYU,

who I might never
see again.

I tell him we were going
to go skateboarding that afternoon,
were going
to go to college together someday,
were going to be friends forever.

I tell him about
my grandparents,
and everything—
even my AWOL Dad.

Once I start talking,
I can't stop.

He listens, sighs,
kicks the sand.
Drinks a beer.
Then another.

YOU'D BETTER GET BACK

before dark, he says.

I've nowhere to go.

In that case, he says, laughing,
pull up a futon.

Eventually,
he falls asleep,
snoring.

I stay there
for a while,
shivering in the cold.

Then I think I fall asleep,
but I'm not sure.

Maybe I'm drunk.

THE MOON ON THE WATER

looks so peaceful.

I want to be
peaceful, too.

Before I know it,
I've stepped
into the sea,
walked farther
and farther out.

Out to where
I cannot hear
the chatter
in my mind.

Out to where
I can only hear
the sound
of the waves.

So loud,
so quiet
at the
same time.

ARM OVER ARM

I keep swimming out.
Right hand
pulling me
toward the moon,
left hand
pushing me
away from land,
as far out as I can.

Then I roll over,
let
myself
go.

The waves move
my floating body
gently,
rock me
here and there.

DON'T KNOW

where I am
or how long
I've been here
when I hear
splashing near me.

Is it a shark?
A whale?
A spirit?

Red-faced,
weather-beaten,
water dripping
from face and hair,
someone rises up
in front of me,
shoots his arms
up from the water.

What are you
trying to do?
he shouts,
yanks me up,

hauls me back,
shakes me dry
as if I were
a strand
of seaweed.

TARO NISHI, THAT CRAZY NINJA,

hauls me
toward the shore,
shoves me down
onto the sand.

Then he
kicks me
hard,
because
he can.

WHAT DID YOU COME HERE FOR?

I yell.
You! I'm here for you!
he shouts,
shaking off the water.

What?
I kick him back.
He pushes me down.
I push him back.

And then we're wrestling
on the sand,
like we did
in the school yard
and in the shelter
and on the soccer field—
like we've done
so many times before.

Get out of here!
Leave me alone!

Idiot! he says.
He's cursing
and shouting
and I'm cursing
and shouting.

Let me go! I yell,
take off running
again.

He comes after me,
grabs my soaking sleeve,
pulls me down.

There's nowhere to go,
he says.

She saw you pack your bag . . .
couldn't let you do
something so stupid.

Who? I ask.
Keiko. She asked me to
find you.

Keiko? This is about Keiko?
What's it to you? I sputter.

Nothing to me, but . . . , he says,
looks into my eyes.

I stop fighting.
I take a breath.
I look around
at the ocean and the ruined land.

The ocean can't bring back
my mom
and I can't bring back
the past,
but it's just Taro's bad luck
that bringing
me back
helps Keiko,
and that's what he wants to do.
Now I get it.

Throwing me over his shoulders
like he slung
Keiko after the quake,
Taro carries me
back to town.

And for once
in my life,
I let him.

OLD MAN SATO IS AT THE PIER

washing down his nets,
like always.

He waves his wrinkled hand,
veins like maps on his skin.

Oi! Come here!

Taro puts me down.

If you've got
more bad news, I say,
I don't want
to hear it.

Old Man Sato smiles,
shakes his head.
No more news.
This story's old.

He motions to his paint-peeled boat
anchored just offshore.

Have a seat, he says.

THERE'S A SAYING IN COASTAL TOWNS—

inochi tendenko—
save your own life first.

A long time ago,
if you wanted to
marry someone from the coast,
the elders asked:

"If a tsunami came,
who would you save first?
Your wife and child,
or yourself?"

"If you can't save yourself first,"
they said,
"you can't marry anyone here."
They'd lived through a tsunami,
knew its full power.

It's true.
If you can't save your own life,
the town will disappear.

And if that happens,
the future, too,
will disappear.

So don't you dare
feel guilty for being alive,

Old Man Sato says,
looking from me to Taro
and back again.

We've got the future
to build.

KEIKO RUSHES TO THE AUDITORIUM DOOR,

eyes red, face flushed.

Where've you been?
Are you all right?
Thank god!

He's fine, Taro says,
eyebrows up.
We're fine.

I hold his gaze, nod.
Taro looks at Keiko
and back at me.
Her face lights up.
My lips crack into a grin—
first one in months.

She likes me!
And Taro is right.
I'm an idiot
for not noticing
until now.

KENJI CAME BACK, TOO,

Keiko says.
He wants to know
if you're going
to New York.

Huh? Kenji?
New York? I mumble.

He needs an answer.
I'd totally forgotten.
Keiko glances to the back
of the auditorium,
where a tall, broad-shouldered man
is sitting at a folding table,
drinking tea.
When he sees me,
he waves,

stands up,
walks my way.

I'M KENJI, HE SAYS,

holding out his hand.
You must be Kai.

Uh . . .
I want to pull away,
but he doesn't
give me a chance,
just pumps my hand
up and down
American-style.

Then he tells me
that kids from the devastated towns
will go to New York
to meet kids
who lost their parents in 9/11,
when hijacked airplanes
crashed into the World Trade Center
ten years ago.

WILL YOU COME? HE ASKS,

soft black eyes
looking straight at me.

I don't know, I say.
Shin needs me here.
And Guts.

I look around,
see past the window,
where the kids are outside
with Taro,
kicking the flat ball around.
Kind of ruins my argument.

I've already talked to them,
Keiko says.
They think you should go.

Kenji nods, agrees.
Those kids in New York
have been through something like
what you're going through.
They might know how you feel, he says.

KENJI KNOWS, TOO.

He was a baby
when the Second World War
broke out.
His parents sent him
to the countryside for safety,
like so many others.

Like so many others,
he lost his mom and dad
when Tokyo was destroyed.

He grew up
in an orphanage.
For a long time,
he felt sorry
for himself.
But then he got tired
of feeling helpless,
tried to help others.

If I hadn't suffered,
I wouldn't have
known or cared
how those kids felt,
he says.

But since I went
through it,
I know how tough it is
to come out the other side.
That's where I want to be for others.

KEIKO WATCHES,

listening.
I watch her,
see the streak
of dirt on her nose,
a hundred freckles
I've never noticed.
And then I see her dad
in her face,
the way people
saw my dad
in mine.

Coach Inoue—
who believed in me,
stood up for me,
gave me a chance
before I blew it.

I know Keiko's
counting on me
to go for her,
for all of us.
Will you come?
Kenji asks.

I TAKE DEEP BREATHS,

try to remember the calming steps
Coach taught me.

1. Take three deep breaths.
2. Watch your thoughts for five counts.
3. Think of what someone you trust would do.

I get through #1 and #2,
get stuck on #3.
What would Mom do? I wonder.
She would go.
She taught me perseverance—
that's how she lived.

You put a shell in the water
and you wait.
Sometimes an oyster grows;

sometimes it doesn't.
But you lower the line
just the same.

What would Dad do?
I ask myself.
I thought Dad taught me
how to follow
my dreams.

But now I see
that what he really
taught me
was how
to run away.

If I say no,
I'll be
no different
from him.

So I say,
   Y
     e
       s.

KEIKO JUMPS UP,

gives me a hug—
my first hug—
then shouts my name.

Shin and his dad
come over,
ask what's going on.

Kenji tells them
I'm going to New York.
Wow! Cool!
Shin says,
grinning wide.

Shin's dad
puts his arm
around me.
Good for you! he says.

This time,
I don't push
him away.

WE LEAVE SEPTEMBER FIFTH,

Kenji says,
hands me a
Japanese-English dictionary
with a worn
brown leather cover.

This was mine
when I was your age.

I take it in both hands,
carefully, as the pages
are coming apart.
I bow low and long.

Good luck! he says in English.
I'm gonna need it, I reply.

THREE WEEKS TO ENGLISH

feels like three minutes
but it's all I've got.

Maybe it's better that way.
I'll be so busy getting ready to go

that I won't have enough time
to talk myself out of it.

At night,
I pull the blankets
over my head,
wrap my mouth
around words
I used to speak
when I was little.

Hello,
Good-bye,
Nice to meet you,
My name is Kai.

I'm Japanese.
Then I correct myself:
Half Japanese. . . .

And then some words
I never thought
I'd say:

I lost my mother, too.

STILL WANT TO BELIEVE

I'll see her once more,
eat her crunchy *kaki furai*,
watch stupid game shows on TV,
laugh together again.

O-BON* WILL BE HERE SOON—

the summer festival
when the spirits come back
to visit Earth.
The shrine is cleaned,
the paths are cleared,
the lanterns hung.

On that day, I force myself
to join the festival.
With so many spirits
traveling so far
to come home,
how could
I not take

---

* *O-Bon* is the festival of the dead, when the spirits come back to the
earth to visit with the living. It is celebrated in the seventh month of
the year in the solar calendar (July) in some areas, and in August (to
coincide with the old lunar calendar) in others.

a few small steps
to go out
and greet them?

FIREFLIES LIGHT UP THE SKY,

villagers gather around
the red *torii**
wearing bright kimonos
donated by strangers.

Grandmothers in *yukata*.†
Young mothers
with newborn babies
on their backs—
three generations
dancing,
feet tapping
the same land
our families
have stood on
for generations.

---

* *torii*—the gateway to a Shinto shrine, marking the entrance to a sacred space, made of two red or orange vertical columns and two crosspieces

† *yukata*—bright cotton summer kimonos

I WATCH THE WOMEN SWAY TO

*"Tohoku Ondo"**—
the dance Mom always loved,
arms swinging gracefully
as she drew
Mount Fuji in the air.

Clap clap clap

You and I love Tohoku
as we were born
and raised here. . . .

Arms up to the right,
arms up to the left,

palms together,
step back,
spin.

Dancing to this ballad
is the very
breath of life,

....

* *Tohoku*—region located in northeastern Honshu, the largest island of
Japan. *Ondo*—a type of Japanese folk music.

carrying
the spirit of
our mother
back to us.

Feeling the
unbreakable spirit
of Tohoku.

Feeling Mom,
Ojiichan, and
Obaachan
with me
now.

秋

Fall

Ascend

WISH MOM WERE HERE

the day Kenji comes to get me,
wish she were here
to see me off
to New York.
Wish she were standing
next to Keiko,
who is standing beside
Shin's family,
Old Man Sato,
Aki-*sensei*,
Principal Kunihara,
Guts and the soccer kids—
all gathered to
wish me well.

Even Taro Nishi
gives me a Samurai Blue T-shirt,
says *Forget it*,
when I say—

for the first time ever—
Thank you.

DRIVING WITH THE TOP DOWN,

breeze in our hair
passing town
after town
along the
coast.

Kesennuma—
with its giant
red ship stranded
on concrete.

Minamisanriku—
where a thousand origami cranes
hang in memory
of those no longer here.

Ishinomaki—
where the shell
of a building remains,
a monument to the girl
who stayed

on the rooftop
warning everyone
by megaphone:
Take cover!
Tsunami's on the way!

In the distance, Matsushima,
its pine forests
still standing, as
nearby islands
had blocked the tsunami's path.

Makes me remember
our pines are almost all down—
hope we plant some soon.

TWO OTHER COASTAL KIDS

meet us at Sendai airport—
another guy my age, Masa,
and Tomo, a girl two years younger.

We drink tea, munch *senbei*,
talk about what to buy
our New York hosts—

furoshiki wrapping cloths
or *tenugui* hand towels?

So nice to think about
what to give
instead of
what's been
taken away.

ON THE PLANE,

the cabin lights go out
but I can't sleep.

In science we learned
that nothing is solid,
that everything is energy,
that atoms are made of
quarks and photons,
and that humans
are made of atoms.

If what we are—
me and Shin and Keiko—
is energy,
what about

my mom
and grandparents?

What are they
made of
now that
they're not here?

MAYBE THEY CAN HEAR

these thoughts
in my head.

Maybe they can feel
what I'm feeling.

I want to believe
that up here
in the sky
I'm closer to them
somehow.

DON'T EVEN NOTICE

I've closed my eyes
until we're about to touch ground
in America.

America!
On the street
the taxi hurtles
into Manhattan,
while Tomo, Masa, and I
slide on the backseat,
bumping into each other.
We apologize,
say *sumimasen*.

Kenji laughs.
You're in America! he says.
You don't have to
keep saying
I'm sorry.

STRANGE MUSIC
....

streams from our
careening taxi
and from the city streets.

Honking horns,
people shouting,
laughing, talking in

many languages—
welcome to New York.

We sleep for hours
at the hotel, wake up
just before we meet
our hosts.

TOM'S A BIG, TALL MAN

with a barrel chest,
like a wrestler.

Fia is short, fit, and sparkly,
her eyes emerald green.
They bring
brown paper bags
filled with warm bagels
smeared with cream cheese
for breakfast.

We sit in a circle
on the floor,
eating and telling
our stories.

Tom's mom and dad
were in the Twin Towers
when the plane hit.

He was fourteen then,
angry for a long time after.
He dropped out of school
and started working
at a youth center—
now he's the manager.

Fia's dad was a firefighter,
a first responder
on the scene—

their parents
were never found.

Fia was seventeen,
the same age
I am now,
and had lost her mother
just a year before.

She wondered how
she'd go on.

But here I am, she says.
Now she's a social worker.

IT TOOK A LONG TIME

to recover, says Tom,
then adds,
I'm still recovering.
Fia says it's not
always easy,
but every day
before she goes to bed,
she thinks about
all the good things in her life—
her husband, her aunt and uncle,
her teachers, and her cat,
whose name is Sushi.
Really!

WHERE WERE YOU WHEN THE QUAKE STRUCK?

they want to know.
For Masa, Tomo, and me,
it's the first time
we've talked about
3/11 with anyone.

But the words
pour out.

It's easier to talk
to strangers
here on foreign soil,
and English ,
gives me freedom.
Even if I make mistakes,
it doesn't seem
to matter.

I TELL THEM THINGS

I've never even
told Shin.

I show them the
sea-warped picture
of Mom and Dad,
tell them
how Dad left us,
could never seem
to find his place.

Even when my
words don't fit together perfectly,
I think they understand.

MASA TELLS THEM

how when the earthquake struck,
he was coming home from school
and tried to get his brother
from kindergarten.
He never made it.
All the roads were blocked
with moms in cars
trying to get their kids.

They all
got swept away
in the waves.

Kenji translates,
a lump in his throat.

I TALK ABOUT KEIKO,

how she froze under the desk,
how I couldn't help her.

I tell them
she doesn't remember
anything after that.

I tell them about
climbing the tree,
getting thrown
out of the water,
and how the principal
took me to the junior high,
which became our shelter.

I tell them that Taro
pulled me from the ocean
and that
I wanted to die. . . .

I was scared, I say.
It's okay to be scared,
Tom replies.

If you weren't scared,
you wouldn't be human,
you wouldn't be brave.

What do you mean? I ask.

If you were fearless,
you wouldn't
need to overcome it.

Bravery means being scared
and going forward
anyway, Fia says.
That's courage.

I start to cry,
and that's when
Tom wraps his arms
around me for a hug.

When I tense up,
he reassures me.
You're in New York,
he says.
Hugs are what
we do.

SHO GA NAI—IT CAN'T BE HELPED.

I hate those words,
Tomo says
when it's her turn
to share.

Fia asks her why.

That's what everyone says.
They say quakes and tsunamis
are a natural cycle of the Earth,
just a fact of life.
But we're part of the Earth, too.
Right?

I nod, remembering
Mrs. Tanaka's science lectures
on overfishing, factory farming,
greenhouse gas emissions,
the ones I used to tune out,
whispering to Ryu, *Blah blah blah.* . . .

Now I wonder if humans really *are*
causing rains and floods,

quakes, tornadoes, and hurricanes,
making birds fall from the sky, whales beach.

I wonder about the reactors leaking
radioactive particles into the air and sea.
And I wonder what will happen
when the particles drift far away.

TOMO WAS AT HER FAMILY'S STORE,

unpacking cabbage.
Her mom and dad
ran home to get
her grandparents
and were never
seen again.

We all remember
exactly where we were
and what we were doing
when our lives
changed forever.

9/11 and 3/11 are so different,
two separate disasters—

but maybe they're also
the same, Tomo says.

How so? Kenji asks.

Each one changed
our country forever.

We all nod,
understanding.

Losing your parents
is the same
everywhere.

MAYBE THAT'S THE SILVER LINING,

if there can be such a thing, Kenji says—
to see the connections,
to get perspective.

When we help
each other,
we become bigger
than ourselves.

Mom said the same thing,
I remember,
she always
told me
not to play small.

I even had the words
of Endo Mamoru*
hanging over my desk:

Dekinai to omottara, dekinai.
Dekiru to omoeba, nandemo dekiru.

If you think something's impossible,
you can't do it.
But if you think something's possible,
you can do anything.

I used to look at it every day
before going out to play.

When did I forget?

....

* Captain of the soccer team Raimon from the anime *Inazuma Eleven*

I KEEP THE WORDS IN MIND

when we go to
Ground Zero.

I don't know if I'm ready,
I say to Kenji
as we ride the subway
downtown.

He nods, then replies,
I don't know if I'll ever
be ready.
But we'll do it
together.

THE GRANITE HOLES

where the towers once were
are reflecting pools.
We stand in silence
with our new friends.

People crouch low
to kiss the names of loved ones
etched into bronze,

touch the edges
remembering
fathers, mothers,
sisters, brothers, aunts, uncles,
children. . . .

They leave tokens
next to the names,
drape blue entrance ribbons
over the bronze panels,
place flowers and flags nearby.

Not so different
from the way
I offered *Obaachan*
pumpkin and mochi
across an ocean,
sending her spirit
to Nirvana.

Tom sweeps his fingers
over the monument,
touching his parents' names.

A NINE-YEAR-OLD

speaks from the podium,
talks to her father,
who she never met,
because she was still
in her mom's belly
when he died.

Though she never knew him,
she says she loves him,
loves her father
for loving
the idea of having her.

Did my dad
love the idea
of having me,
too?

I TAKE THE BUSTED CELL PHONE

from my pocket,
place it
on the wall.

At first I think
I'll just
set it there,

but then
after a while
I decide
to leave it
alongside
the precious things
my friends
have left behind.

Mom's last words
aren't inside it
anymore,
I know.
They're inside me.

I love you, Kai.

LEAVING THE MONUMENT

we pass the pear tree
pulled
from the rubble,
nurtured back to health.

A lone survivor,
just like the black pine
in my town.

IN THE MIDDLE OF BROADWAY

I know
I have to do
what I couldn't do
before.

I know
I don't want
to be small
anymore.

Think I'm ready
to
find
my dad.

WHEN I TELL TOM, HE DOESN'T ASK

why I waited,
just says:
Let's get a move on!

The address
on the package Dad sent
so many years ago
is still
seared into my brain—
How could I forget 28 King Street?
I even remembered the apartment number.

No time to lose!

WE SPLIT OFF FROM THE GROUP,

walk uptown,
pass a fire station
with photos along the wall,
flowers on the floor
for all those lost.

We take Church Street
to Sixth Avenue,

turn at King,
and suddenly
we're standing
at the door.

Tom nods,
urges me
toward it.

I freeze,
can't move.
He nods.
I step forward, but
my fingers stop
midair.
They shake
like my knees.

Can't ring that bell.

What if he answers?
What if he doesn't?

TAKE YOUR TIME, TOM SAYS.

I sit down on the stoop.
He sits down next to me.

Just sixty years ago,
this wouldn't
have been possible, he says,
shakes his head.

Huh? I say, not understanding.

Back then, our two countries
didn't speak.

Oh. Back then, I say.

I'm not sure what he's getting at.

Yeah. We were once enemies.
Now we're friends.

Yeah, I say. *That's true.*

And then I think
I get it:
Things change.

THINGS CHANGE.

People change.
I've changed.

I stand up,
walk to the door,
push my fingertip
into the little
brass button,
inhale,
ring the bell,
hold it
for what seems like
forever,
exhale.

NO ANSWER.

Isn't Dad there?
Or his wife?

I ring again.
Then again.
Nothing.

It's Sunday, Tom says,
standing up,
brushing
off his jeans.
Maybe they're just out
for the day.

I try to stand up,
but I can't.

I don't want to leave,
I say.

Okay. We can stay here
for a while then,
Tom says, sitting
back down again.

He crosses his arms
over his chest and brings
his knees to his chin.

It gets chilly
as night
starts to fall.

I think we'd better go, Tom finally says.
I don't want to leave, I say again.
I know, but your father isn't here, Tom replies,
putting a hand on my shoulder.

I mean, I don't want to leave New York, I explain.
I can't believe I came all the way
and didn't even
find my father.

Is that really why you came?
he asks.
I don't know, I reply.

I think I know, he says.

I breathe in again,
think it through.

I thought I came
to get away,
but now I'm not so sure.

MAYBE DAD LEFT THIS APARTMENT
YEARS AGO

like he left Japan—
without a trace.

You tried, Tom says,
standing up
from the stoop.
Nothing more you can do here.

But just in case
Dad comes back soon,
he urges me
to leave a note.

With my best English
penmanship
I write:

THIS IS KAI,
YOUR SON
FROM JAPAN.
PLEASE CONTACT ME.

I write my email
and my address

at the school.
Then I fold it like an
origami frog.

It's my little joke.

Frog is *kaeru* in Japanese.
Kaeru also means
"come back."

Just in case,
I stick it
under the door.

That's it,
Tom says.
You've done
what you
could do.

But I'm not so sure.

There must be *something* more I can do.
Have you looked on Facebook?
Tom asks.

I don't tell him I've lurked
around Dad's profile before,
too chicken to connect.

But somehow
I think he knows.
Tom hands me his phone.

Okay, I say,
bite my lip,
type in Dad's name,
hit Search.

A blurry photo
of a middle-aged guy
with shoulder-length blond hair,
tanned skin,
a few wrinkles around the eyes
comes up.
He's wearing
a plaid flannel shirt
and jeans,
standing at an outdoor café.

Is that him?

Haven't seen him in seven years.
Haven't pulled up his page in a while,
looks like the picture's changed.

Is that my dad?
Could be anyone's dad.

Dad. I'm here in New York.
I type in the message box.
*I've only got
one more day.
Please contact me.
Kai.*

FIRST THING IN THE MORNING

When Tom shows up,
I use his phone
to check Facebook
and email.

Nothing.
I have to let it go.
It's our last day
in New York,

and I want
to enjoy it.

(And it's my birthday,
though I haven't
told anyone.)

Tom and Fia take us to Coney Island
for hot dogs,
give us I ♥ NY T-shirts
and little Statue of Liberty
souvenirs, the kind
that rain snow
when you shake them.

Kenji treats us all to sushi lunch,
and we give them our
gifts from Japan,
teach them how to fold and wrap—
they love them all.

We exchange email addresses,
promise to stay in touch,
maybe come again.

IT'S OUR LAST NIGHT HERE—

Kenji says we have to celebrate
my birthday in style.
What? Who told you that?
A little birdie,
he says with a big smile.

Keiko!

That's how we end up
eating oysters on the half shell
at the best oyster bar in New York,
where waiters in starched white shirts
and crisp black pants
pull out our chairs.

Mom would have laughed
to see where her
humble oysters
could have ended up.

Slurping the slimy lumps
I used to hate,

I'm surprised
to taste the ocean,
surprised at just
how good they are.

Arrive

AS WE FLY BACK OVER THE PACIFIC

the ocean looks so calm,
so blue and clear,
from high above.

The flight attendants
hand out newspapers.
I open *The Japan Times*,
read about a 9/11 memorial in Tokyo,
people gathered to remember
twenty-three Fuji Bank workers
lost in the World Trade Center—
twelve were Japanese.

Their families laid flowers
in front of a glass cabinet
encasing a small section
of steel from Ground Zero.

Bent but not broken,
the article says,
like the human spirit.

I used to think
stuff like that was corny.
I don't anymore.

SHIN AND HIS FAMILY

are waiting at Sendai airport,
English sign held high.
We're proud of you, Kai!
So un-Japanese
it makes me laugh.

I tell them about
the subway
and the hot dogs
and the pretzels
and the horse-drawn carriages
in Central Park.
I tell them about Ground Zero
and the grown-up
"survivors" I met

who were once kids
just like us.
And the oysters.

Next time you're taking me,
Shin says.
Definitely! I say in English,
giving him a high five as
we walk toward
their borrowed car.

WHEN I SAY GOOD-BYE,

Kenji gives me a
birthday present,
to keep in touch—
a new cell phone
with his number
already in it.

WE DRIVE UP THE COAST,

pass the lone pine
standing like a flagpole,
bare and branchless

but proud,
rising from the crater
of my town.

Someone wrapped it
in braids of ceremonial white rope.
Strips of white paper
flutter from its
curved trunk.

70,000 pines on the coast—
now only one left.

173 years ago
it was just a seed.

It's a miracle.

IF I HADN'T CLIMBED IT,

I wouldn't
have survived.

That's a miracle,
too.

I want to be
like that tree,
deep roots
making it strong,
keeping it
standing tall.

IN TOWN,

Old Man Sato's at the docks
tending to his boats
like always.

Tadaima! I'm home!
I call out from the car window,
just like I said every day
arriving home from school,
where Mom was waiting.

Okaerinasai,
he shouts and waves.
Welcome home.

AT THE SHELTER,
KEIKO IS KNITTING BOOTIES

for the new babies,
like *Obaachan*
used to do.

I raise my eyebrows.
When did you start that?

Life goes on,
she says, and smiles.

Then she shows me
piles of new futons,
beds, cookware, and tables,
refrigerators,
couches, and stoves
we'll use
in our new homes.

We're starting over.

And then I do
what I've always
wanted to do:

I lean in
toward Keiko
and kiss her.

And she
kisses
me back.

IT GETS EVEN BETTER

when a Japanese lady in Hawaii
tracks me down out of the blue,
says she's found
my old soccer ball—
the one from Dad.
What? Hawaii?

She's married to an American man,
found it while
walking on the beach.

She could understand
the *kanji*,*
the well-wishes

---

* *kanji*—a Japanese writing system consisting of ideograms

from my friends
and Coach.

Can something like that really
happen?
How crazy is that?

Though I don't even know her
she promises
to send it
back.

Shin swears
it's a sign,
says if the ball
comes back,
we've got to be
ready to use it—
we've got
to give it
a home.

We've got to
trust this sign,
he insists.

We've got to
listen.

Okay, I say.
I'm listening.

WE TEACH THE KIDS

how to feint and head,
strike and trap.

They say they
don't want to stop
once they move out
of the shelter,
move to temporary housing.

Do we have to stop?

I talk to Principal Kunihara
and Aki-*sensei*.

I'm dreaming up
a plan.

GUTS FOLLOWS ME EVERYWHERE,

showing me his moves.
I guess he missed me.
I guess I missed
him, too.

Now he knows
how to kick
with the instep,
not the toes,
how to juggle
as if catching the ball,
not kicking it,
how to see the openings
on the field
before shooting a pass.
He knows
what I myself forgot:
the ball is your friend.

EVERY DAY WE CLEAR THE LAND

above school,
tearing up weeds,
sifting out rocks,
leveling the ground.

Guts and his gang
show up with brooms
and rakes.

Village women
untangle torn fishing nets,
mend the holes.

Old Man Sato
strings them up
between bamboo poles,
and soon
we've got
our goals.

Even Taro helps.

We use
what we have.

EVERY DAY WE PRACTICE

until our legs ache.

I do my best
just in case
Shin's theory is true.

If my ball
somehow
finds its way
to me,
can Dad
be far behind?

And maybe even
Mom?
Is it too much to hope for?

Will the people I love
come back?

ANYTHING CAN HAPPEN.

Shin's dad, Aki-*sensei*,
and Principal Kunihara

say I'm good at soccer—
better than good.

They think we can even
form a team.

They say since I speak English,
I could play anywhere
in the world—
Brazil, Spain, England,
like Yuto Nagatomo,
who plays in Italy,
Keisuke Honda,
who went all the way to Russia
and Italy too,
and Shinji Kagawa,
who moved to England and
Germany.

It could happen, Shin says.
With your talent and the language,
you can do it,
Shin's dad agrees.

But it's been so long,
and I'm a wreck, I say.

I wonder if I can
get my skills back
after so many years.

But they believe it,
so I start to believe it, too.
My mind remembered English.
Will my body remember soccer?

THE QUAKE MOVED THE EARTH

ten inches
on its axis.

I guess
I shifted,
too.

WORD GETS OUT

about our team
playing on a crumbling pitch—
Seaside Eleven,
inspired by the anime
I used to love.

People all over Japan
send shoes and socks,
shin protectors,
jackets and clothes,
enough sports drinks
and snacks to last a year.

Kenji tells
our friends
in America,
who tell their friends
in England
and Europe,
who collect enough money
to buy us uniforms.

A Tokyo sports store
sends us soccer
balls and pumps.

A coach from
another town
arranges our
first match.

Feels like everyone
in the world
is cheering us on.

ELEVEN PLAYERS ON EACH SIDE—

the day of our first match.
Me, Shin, Guts, Taro Nishi,
and a handful of kids
from the shelter
against an inland team—
the Phoenix.

We make a line,
bow down deep
to thank the grounds,
like we always did
in practice,
like Coach Inoue
taught us.

My knees shake,
and I take
deep breaths
and wonder if

I'm going to faint.
But then
the whistle
blows.

Go!

MY EYES LOCK ON TARO,

who passes
me the ball.
It goes wide,
but I latch on to it,
dribble it
down the pitch fast
until the Phoenix sideback
swipes it away from me,
his foot like a sword.

Guts barrels in,
takes the ball away,
but they block
us at every turn—
we can't get
near the goal.

Finally, Guts lands a nice clean pass
at Shin's feet
just when he has an opening,
Shin slams it toward the net—
our chance!

But the Phoenix keeper
gets there first.
Big as a sumo wrestler
and strong like Ryu,
he beats the ball
back down,
slaps it away.

Then the Phoenix midfielder
snags it,
races down the field
to the goal,
tings a shot
off the crossbar.
Safe!

But the striker
heads the ball
high into the net—
how did that happen?

0–1.

At center circle again,
we start,
cluster too close,
fall apart
trying to stay alive.

#3 steals the ball from Taro,
Shin steals it back,
sees an open road,
passes it to me.
I kick it in.

Offside!

The goal doesn't count.

Don't mind, don't mind,
Aki-*sensei* calls out.
I try to keep
my head up
for the team.

Ten seconds to halftime.
We fight off

more Phoenix attacks—
then Guts sails one
between the keeper's legs,
straight
into the center.

Woo-hoo!
Woo-hoo!

1–1!

Go, Seaside Eleven!
the crowd calls out.
Halftime
whistle blows.

BEFORE I EVEN SEE HER,

I know she's there.
Keiko!
She's come outside!
And what is she carrying?
My old ball.

It just arrived,
she says,
tossing it over.

What? No way!
I catch it,
cradle it
to my chest.
Someone even cleaned it,
pumped it up.
The seams are unraveled,
but it will still work—
it *has* to still work!

Shin gives me a thumbs-up.
I knew it! he says.

I roll my eyes.
But maybe he's right.
Maybe it is
a sign.

WHEN HALFTIME ENDS,

I take position
with my old ball
just like I did
hundreds of times before.

The whistle blows
for kickoff.
I pass it to Shin,
run full speed ahead.
He slices it back,
but a Phoenix defenseman
sweeps it away.

Shin shouts my name.
I see their striker
rushing toward
the goal.

Gotta stop him!

I deepen my breath,
run straight
for the player,
straight for that ball.

Burning my gaze into the ball,
I slide my foot
beneath the striker's
foot,
swoop my feet around

the ball to
make it mine.

Keeping it on my toes,
I turn around,
feint left,
fly down the pitch,
shoot a pass
to Shin,
head toward
the goal.
He traps the ball,
volleys it back to me,
and I launch it
at the net,
but it's too wide—
No!

Then midair it curves
in the wind,
like it has a mind
of its own,
heads straight
into the net.

What?

The keeper jumps high
and the ball soars
over his glove,
out of reach.

YES!

Goal!

Keiko's calling out my name
and everyone cheers
and high-fives
and I'm soaring, too.

2–1

Not much time left
when Guts
sticks out his hand
in a mash-up,
and the ref yells,

Foul!

The Phoenix
get a free kick.

#6 slams the ball
past our keeper,
just barely into the corner
but into the net
just the same.

2–2.

THEN SOMETHING CHANGES—

I feel it in the way
the air shifts
like it does
when someone you like
comes into a room,
changing
everything.

Keiko left the shelter,
but that's not
the only thing. . . .

I HEAR HIM BEFORE I SEE HIM,

calling out my name
as if he's always done that

from the sidelines.
I look up, see him
standing in the bleachers,
smiling, waving,
beaming
at me.

Those eyes—
deep blue, shining,
though his face
is older now.

What the—?
How the—?
Too many questions,
no time to ask.
Clock's ticking.
We need a miracle.
Wish Ryu were here.

I WAVE, AND DAD WAVES BACK.

Have to keep my focus.
Breathing.
Running.

One foot
in front
of the
other,
have to
be on
my game.

SOMETHING TAKES OVER

and it's just
the boys and me
dribbling and
passing the ball,
just like Dad
and I used to do,
like nothing
ever happened—
I mean like
nothing bad
ever happened.

Everything goes quiet
like it did inside
the water,
but this time

I know
I'll come out
the other side.

Flying down the pitch
I shoot the ball
toward the net,
putting everything I've got
behind it—

WHAM!

The keeper
catches it in
his arms.

No way!

The Phoenix take
possession
and it looks like we're sunk. . . .

But just when I think
we're done for,
Taro appears
out of nowhere

like the ninja
that he is,
gets the ball,
and fires a long shot
all the way
in.

Goal!

3–2.

Whistle blows,
twice short,
once long—
tweet tweet
tweeeeeet.

Taro does a backflip,
we slap high fives
around the team.

After losing
so much,
our team,
our town,
has won!

newspaper reporters want to talk to us—
TV stations, too.

All I can see
is my dad,
and Keiko
behind him,
cheering.

He's pushing his way up
to the front of the crowd,
pushing his way
to me.

He wraps his arms around me
and I hug him
right back
(Thank you, Tom!),
as if we've done
this every day
for years.
As if
he never left.

REPORTERS COME CLOSER,

ask for a statement.
I tell them
to talk to Guts.
I tell them
to talk to the people
who donated
all the stuff
that made
our game possible.

I tell them
to talk to
the village women
and the fishermen
and Old Man Sato
and all the people
in the town
and all over the world
who cheered us on.

I say this team
is dedicated
to my mom
and grandparents

and to all the kids
who've lost someone they love
to a quake or a tsunami,
to hunger
or sickness
or war.

I say it's dedicated
to our little coastal town
and to all the other towns
in the world
struck by disaster.
The ones that never
make the news.

WE LINE UP TO BOW

low to the field,
thanking the spectators,
thanking our town.
Arigatou gozaimasu!*
we shout in unison.

* *Arigatou gozaimasu!*—Thank you very much!

Arigatou gozaimasu!
Arigatou gozaimasu!

THEN DAD'S NEXT TO ME

and I'm next to him,
taller than him—
not a little boy
anymore.

He says he's proud of me
for helping to make the team,
but I don't think I've done
anything special.

You'd have
done it, too, I say,
if it was your town.

Anyone would.

GUTS RUNS UP TO GIVE ME FIVE.

I push my palm into his,
then push my old ball

into his arms.
Here. It's yours! I say.
He tries to give it back.
No. For you!
I wrap his fingers around it,
make him take it for good.
Hope his wishes come true.

Mom was right:
If you love something,
set it free.

DAD AND I GO OUT FOR RAMEN

at a temporary
ramen stand.
We slurp the warm noodles
loudly,
just like we always did
after games.

Except this time
Dad doesn't have a beer
like he always did.

His words come out in a rush
I struggle to keep up with him.

I'm sorry
it took so long.
I came as soon
as I could.

But . . . , I say, not understanding.
It took months.
Why?

He says he went into *rehab*—
but I don't know
the English word.
Rehabiri?—Rehabilitation?
Were you hurt?

He tells me what it means,
says his second wife left him
and he fell apart.

When the tsunami struck,
he wanted to come here,
but he couldn't face me,
couldn't face himself.

The tsunami woke him up—
no more excuses.

I lost you once,
didn't want to lose you
again, he says.

I want to say,
Too little, too late,
but I know he did
the best he could.
And he's my dad,
after all.
He's all I have.

I had to get clean.
Once I decided to come,
I wanted it to be
a surprise.

Well, it definitely was,
I say.

He says he's sorry,
so sorry
about Mom.

Then he puts his head
in his hands
and I put my hand
on his back,
and it's *me*
who's comforting
him.

It's okay, I say.
You're here now.

DAD STAYS TO HELP ME

arrange my new room
at Shin's family's
temporary house—
fresh tatami mats,
brightly painted walls,
brand-new bookcase,
brand-new desk,
brand-new pencils
and sharpeners,
plenty of erasers,
notebooks, and a lamp.

I place the photo
of Dad and Mom

on my dresser
with my diploma.

I place the snow globe from New York
next to the rice bowl
I picked out from the rubble
of our house.

I tell him how
Aki-*sensei* made us promise
to meet at the school
when we're twenty-one,
on March 11 at 2:46 p.m.,
the exact time
the earthquake hit.

This is the last homework
I'll give you,
he said,
finally breaking down
after finishing the speech
he'd stayed up
all night to write.

PRINCIPAL KUNIHARA HANDED
US OUR DIPLOMAS

one by one
on graduation day,
bowing long and low.

Ours was the only school
to have a graduation,
since volunteers
worked nonstop
to clear away
the mud.

The self-defense forces
found our diplomas
in the debris,
tried to clean them off.

They were torn
and smudged,
but we didn't want
to wash them off.
We wanted to keep them
the way they were.

I TELL DAD THIS

as we walk up
to the shrine.

His guitar is slung
over his shoulder,
just like before.

Soon we're high
above the village
in the forest
where he used to sing.

I still play this old thing,
he says, smiling
as he sits down
on the ground.

He asks if he can play
a song he wrote
for me.

I say *okay*.

His fingers slide
along the strings

just like they always did,
but a little slower.

Time
went by
and the years
began to fly,

but you came
to me
and made
me see
how much
I missed
when I missed
you.

So please
forgive me
and let me be
your dad.

He looks up at me,
then looks down
so I don't see him cry.

I tell him
I'm glad
he came
back.

And then
I use my new cell phone
to take a picture
of the two of us—
Dad and me.

LOOKING AT THE PHOTO

later,
I can see
I look like Dad,
it's true.
I also look
like Mom.
But mainly
I look
like
me.

THAT NIGHT

Dad gives me
a soccer ball—
thermal bound,
the web of fibers
heated to make
a bond so strong
it will never
come apart.

Not old-school style
because stitches
unravel.

I put it by my bed
and sleep soundly
in my new room.

I DREAM OF MOM

in her kitchen,
wearing a striped blue apron,
bangs framing
her heart-shaped face,

dark brown eyes
soft and strong.

I can almost hear
the sound of her palms
cupping rice
as she tossed it
from hand to hand
to make my *onigiri*
perfectly round.

I can almost smell
the salty sea
on her fingers,
that oyster smell
I used to complain of.

I can almost hear
her telling me
that what she loved best
about oysters
was the way some made
a pearl—

when dirt gets into
an oyster shell,

the mother-of-pearl
wraps around it
to create the
treasure inside.

Without the dirt,
there would be
no pearl.

WHEN I WAKE UP

I feel her here with me,
know
that every
morning
she'll live
in me,
rising
like
the sun,
up
from
the sea.

WHEN DAD ASKS IF I'LL GO BACK

to New York with him,
it's like a dream
come true.

Go to New York for good.
Live with my dad.
Leave this town!

It's everything
I've wished for
in the back of my mind
for so many years,
finally coming true.

But now my dream
has changed.

Maybe I went to New York
to find my dad,
but I found myself
instead.

I THINK OF ALL THE PEOPLE HERE—

Shin and Keiko,
Guts and the soccer kids,
Old Man Sato,
even Taro Nishi.

And when I think about
all the things
we've done
to help each other
and to help our town,
I know
I'll stay.

Afterword

I was in Tokyo, Japan, when the Great East Japan Earthquake and Tsunami struck at 2:46 p.m. on March 11, 2011. We were used to quakes, but this one was different. The massive sharp thrust followed by a violent back-and-forth shaking grew in intensity with each second. I ran out of the building I was in. On the street, I watched a skyscraper sway from side to side above me, hoping it would not come down. Strangers huddled together as the pavement rippled and buckled under us like a wave. This kept on for six minutes. What registered as a 7.5 in Tokyo was a 9.0 along the Tohoku coast. We didn't know that yet. We didn't know that minutes after the quake hit, a massive tsunami slammed onto the shore and devastated those ancient seaside towns.

With no way to know if my six-year-old son was okay, I traversed the city by foot as the sky turned red. Dark clouds hung over the horizon. Sudden rain poured down. When I arrived at my son's kindergarten, I discovered that his eighty-year-old grandfather had already walked the two miles to get him. Safely at home, we watched the news in horror as aftershocks kept coming, jolting already-weakened foundations and rattling nerves. My husband arrived home late that night after walking seven hours from work to our home in west Tokyo. News of a nuclear leak had many residents packing up to leave. Thousands of people were killed, and thousands more would never be found. It would be years before life would return to normal.

Though the decision was agonizing, my family and I chose to stay. Japan had given me so much. It was the least I could do to try to give something back. As I watched from the relatively close (but far enough to be "safe") distance of Tokyo, I wanted to write down everything I saw, heard, and experienced. Though I wasn't in the tsunami zone, the very real and constant shaking of the earth was enough to remind me of the magnitude of the experience.

In the coming days, many who stayed mobilized to help their neighbors. The yoga studio I own organized relief to send to Ishinomaki, Minamisanriku, Rikuzentakata, Oshika, and other devastated towns through the extensive efforts of Second Harvest Japan, Animal Rescue Niigata, and Caroline Pover. Animals that were abandoned were rescued by fearless volunteers who went into the irradiated zones. When school started again after spring break, I traveled to Tohoku and volunteered at the temporary housing shelters with Shanti Volunteer Association and YAM Japan. Also, Sun and Moon Yoga's Community Class funds helped open a library in Oshika, a town that was devastated by the tsunami. Now the community can have books to read and a quiet, clean, homey place to enjoy them—and a garden!

Inspired by a young boy I met in the disaster zone, I began a novel about a boy who loves soccer and creates a team to rally his town after the tsunami. Months later, I discovered that exactly this had been done in coastal Onagawa. The team is the Cobaltore Onagawa Football Club. Supporters from all over the world helped in the difficult days following the disaster.

Later, I learned that a soccer ball that had belonged to a teenager in Rikuzentakata washed up in Alaska. Amazingly, the ball was found by a man with a Japanese wife who could read the messages written on it. The couple traced the owner and traveled to Japan to return the ball.

I've based this novel on the events of March 11, 2011, and their aftermath, including the above tales, as well as events surrounding the tenth anniversary of 9/11, but this story is a work of fiction. Kai is not the boy mentioned above, and the town described in this novel is a composite of several coastal towns struck by the disaster. The geography, history, and characters within these pages are solely a work of the imagination, and any errors are the fault of the author.

The author would like to acknowledge the following sources for shedding light on the many events that inspired this book: Peace Boat Japan, Robert Gilhooly's photographs (japanphotojournalist.com), *USA Today* (Monday, September 12, 2011), *The New York Times* (Monday September 12, 2011, story by Anemona Hartocollis), *The Japan Times*, *Time* magazine (story by Kate Springer: newsfeed.time.com/2012/04/24/soccer-ball-lost-in-japan-tsunami-surfaces-in-alaska), and the *Ishinomaki Hibi Shimbun*.

Acknowledgments

I would like to thank Em Bettinger, Eric Korpiel, and Wayne Shaw, who shared their firsthand experiences of their visits to the tsunami areas in interviews conducted in Tokyo from March to September 2011. Special thanks to Lucy Birmingham, Tomoko Kawahara, Ikuhiro Nakamura, Yaeko Yonezawa, Momoyo Yamaguchi, Takuma Kawamura, and the people of Kesennuma for their valiant spirits and open arms. I bow to you.

In June 2011, four Japanese high school students who lost their parents and family members in the tsunami, and university students whose parents had perished in the 1995 Great Hanshin earthquake in Kobe, Japan, flew to New York to raise awareness and money for the children of Tohoku orphaned in the March 11, 2011, disaster. Two American students, one who had lost her father in 9/11 and another who had lost his mother in Hurricane Katrina, joined efforts organized by the Ashinaga ("Daddy Long Legs") NGO. I was deeply inspired by this story of survivors of tragedies in one country reaching out to survivors in another. I took creative liberty in imagining a meeting between children of 3/11 and children of 9/11 culminating in a visit to the National September 11 Memorial on the tenth anniversary of 9/11.

For help with the manuscript at various stages, heartfelt gratitude especially to my writing partner, Colleen Sakurai, and to Toshiko Yanagihara (angel on earth!), Hatsumi Ishikawa, Sylvie Frank, Jill Corcoran, Susan Korman, Linda Gerber, Shoji Koike, and Deni Béchard, and to Holly Thompson, Suzanne Kamata, Mariko Nagai, Naomi Kojima, Ann Slater, Ellen Yaegashira, and Annie Donwerth-Chikamatsu of SCBWI Japan for their editorial feedback and support. Thanks to Liane Wakabayashi for her wonderful map of Kai's town, which helped me visualize his world. Gratitude above all to my agent extraordinaire, Kelly Falconer, and to Phoebe Yeh for her belief in me and for shepherding this book out into the world with her brilliant editing. More thanks to my stellar team at Crown Books for Young Readers—Rachel Weinick for editorial assistance, Alison Kolani and Renée Cafiero for crackerjack copyediting, Deanna Meyerhoff, who asked about 9/11, and designers Ray Shappell and Heather Kelly. I would also like to thank SCBWI for awarding this book a work-in-progress honor at a crucial stage.

Without a strong home base from my husband and son, I would still be huddled in the corner, terrified. Thank you for drawing me out with your light, bravery, and love.

—Leza Lowitz, March 11, 2014

About the Author

Leza Lowitz's writing has appeared in the *New York Times*, the *Huffington Post*, the *Japan Times*, *Shambhala Sun*, *Asian Jewish Life*, and *Best Buddhist Writing of 2011*. She has published over seventeen books, including the APALA Award–winning YA novel *Jet Black and the Ninja Wind*, which she cowrote with her husband, Shogo Oketani, and the bestselling *Yoga Poems: Lines to Unfold By*. Most recently, she is the author of a memoir, *Here Comes the Sun: A Journey to Adoption in 8 Chakras*.

Her awards include the APALA Asian/Pacific American Award for Young Adult Literature; a PEN Syndicated Fiction Award; the PEN Josephine Miles Award for Poetry; grants from the NEA, the NEH, and the California Arts Council; the Japan-US Friendship Commission Prize for the Translation of Japanese Literature from the Donald Keene Center of Japanese

Culture at Columbia University; the Benjamin Franklin Award for Editorial Excellence; and an SCBWI Work-in-Progress Honor for Multicultural Literature.

Leza, an American, lives in Japan with her husband. You can visit her online at lezalowitz.com.